CHOOSE YOUR OWN ADVENTURE®

Kids Love Reading
Choose Your Own Adventure®!

"Thank you for making these books for kids.
I bet kids that haven't read it yet would love it.
All I can say is that I love your books and I
bet other kids would love them too."
Bella Foster, age 8

"These books are really cool. When I get to
the end of the page, it makes me want to
keep going to find out what is going to happen
to me. I get to make my own choices of
what I WANT to happen next."
Bionca Samuel, age 10

"This book was good. I like that I got
to pick how the story went."
Lily Von Trapp, age 7

"I like how you can make up the story,
but it also tells you a story."
Liam Stewart, age 8

"They have a mystery to them that makes it fun to
read. I like being able to solve them my own way."
Gabe Pribil, age 10

Illustrated by Keith Newton
Book design by Peter Holm, Sterling Hill Productions
For information regarding permission, write to:

CHOOSECO
P.O. Box 46
Waitsfield, Vermont 05673
www.cyoa.com

A DRAGONLARK BOOK

ISBN-10: 1-937133-53-2
EAN: 978-1937133-53-5

Published simultaneously in the United States and Canada

Printed in the United States

11 10 9 8 7 6 5 4 3 2 1

CHOOSE YOUR OWN ADVENTURE®

DINO LAB

BY ANSON MONTGOMERY

ILLUSTRATED BY KEITH NEWTON

A DRAGONLARK BOOK

This book is dedicated to paleontologists, geologists, and others who try to unlock the mysteries of the dinosaurs.

And to Lila and Avery.

READ THIS FIRST!!!

WATCH OUT!
THIS BOOK IS DIFFERENT from every book you've ever read.

Do not read this book from the first page through to the last page. Instead, start on page 1 and read until you come to your first choice. Then turn to the page shown and see what happens.

When you come to the end of a story, you can go back and start again. Every choice leads to a new adventure.

Good luck!

Hooray! Today is the day you and your little sister Maria get to go to the Dino Lab. Your aunt Sarah runs the Dinosaur Research Laboratory, but everyone calls it the Dino Lab. Her team of scientists bring dinosaurs back to life from extinction to learn more about them.

You want to bring your dog Homer with you today, but your parents don't think animals are allowed at the lab, so he has to stay home.

When you and Maria arrive at the Dino Lab, you enter through a giant glass door that slides open when you step up to it. You are in a huge room where the scientists conduct dino-experiments. Everyone is wearing a white lab coat.

"Welcome, kids!" Aunt Sarah says when she sees you, giving you both hugs and kisses. You try not to squirm.

Turn to the next page.

2

"This is my second-in-command, Dr. Treeswinger," she says, gesturing to a chimpanzee wearing a lab coat and glasses.

"Pleased to meet you," Dr. Treeswinger says, shaking your hand.

"And this is our guest from Australia, Dr. Finjump," Aunt Sarah says, pointing to a huge tank of water on wheels. Inside the tank of water is a dolphin and a couple of beach balls.

"Maybe Homer could have come with us after all," you whisper to Maria.

"Also pleased to meet you," a voice from a speaker on top of the tank says.

Turn to page 5.

Aunt Sarah leads you outside to an observation deck overlooking the dinosaur habitat. You go through a special air-lock door that keeps the environment just right for the dinos.

Turn to the next page.

"The dinosaur habitat is over 1,000 square miles and has both water and jungle environments," Dr. Treeswinger says. He points to a hazy valley where tall trees grow up from a swampy area. Then one of the trees moves, and you realize that the trees are actually the necks of Brontosauruses!

"Look, Maria! There are the dinos! Long-neckers!"

"It smells funny in here," Maria says, wrinkling her nose.

"This is how Earth's atmosphere used to smell back in the time of the dinosaurs. But we also have to put special chemicals in the air to keep the dinosaurs, especially the meat-eaters, calm," Dr. Treeswinger explains.

You see a young man at the far end of the observation deck. He is wheeling a cart of vials, tubes, and beakers filled with many different colored fluids. He almost trips over his untied shoelace. Dr. Treeswinger points to him and says, "Gerald is our new lab assistant! He is going to release the calming chemicals soon."

Go on to the next page.

Gerald waves and says, "Hey, Dr. Treeswinger! Have I told you how much I love this job? Dinosaurs are WAY more fun than rats!"

"Ah, here come the baby dinos!" your aunt says, pointing down below. "You are in for a real treat!"

"Wow, look! A baby Tyrannosaurus rex and a baby Stegosaurus!" you tell Maria.

"I know," Maria says. "You don't have to tell me what a Pegosaurus is!"

"Scientists didn't know how big baby dinos were before we brought them back from extinction here at the lab," your aunt tells you. "These two are a couple of years old."

They both look as big as elephants.

"Look!" Dr. Treeswinger yells as a huge Pteranodon swoops above your heads. The wind from its wings ruffles your hair. Maria clutches you tightly.

Turn to the next page.

Gerald is so startled that he knocks the entire cart of chemicals over. A cloud of smoke puffs up from the broken bottles. The Pteranodon flies right through the cloud.

"Is everyone okay?" your aunt asks. The cloud of smoke swirls down into the dino habitat. You watch the baby dinos start to jump around like popcorn kernels as they breathe in the smoke.

"The chemicals are making them go crazy instead of calming them down!" Dr. Treeswinger says.

The Pteranodon is flying straight at you! You grab Maria and duck down.

Whoosh! Crash!

The Pteranodon plows straight into the glass window behind you and breaks it wide open. The baby T. rex and the Stegosaurus climb the stairs of the observation deck and escape through the broken window into the Dino Lab! They stomp through the lab, knocking over the computers and Dr. Finjump's tank. The huge automatic doors open, and the baby dinos stomp right out into the parking lot!

Turn to page 10.

"Can you follow the baby T. rex?" your aunt asks you. "It could get into real trouble. I have to help Dr. Finjump."

"Forget the T. rex!" Gerald yells. "The baby Stegosaurus could really hurt someone!"

What should you do?

If you decide to chase after the baby Tyrannosaurus rex, go on to the next page.

If you think going after the baby Stegosaurus is more important, turn to page 44.

"Come on, we have to get the T. rex!" you tell Maria, tugging at her hand.

"Wait," your aunt says and hands you something that looks like a video game controller. "Take this activator—the T. rex is wearing a Sleep Collar. You have to get close for it to work, but it can put the dino to sleep."

You take the activator and run out the automatic doors.

Turn to page 13.

The dinos are no longer in sight. You follow
a path of ripped up dirt, mangled shrubs, and
squashed cars to the park. Kids are running and
yelling, and a jungle gym has been torn apart. A
police officer is trying to get the kids organized.

"Is everyone okay?" Maria asks the police officer.

"The T. rex ate a couple of swans," she says.
"But no one else is hurt. They're just scared. The
dino ran off toward the zoo. Ask the zookeepers to
help you—they are used to wild animals."

You are about to head to the zoo when you see
your dog Homer over by a trash can.

"Homer! You found us!" you shout, and Homer
barks back. "Come on, we're headed to the zoo!"

Turn to page 15.

You and Maria race to the zoo as fast as you can.

All of the animals in the zoo are going crazy. Birds are squawking, baboons are hooting, elephants are trumpeting, and lions are roaring. Where is Homer? You thought he was following you. Then you see the T. rex jump over the moat onto the tiger island habitat. It grabs the huge piece of meat that was supposed to be the tigers' dinner.

The tigers growl and back off.

Turn to page 17.

"We need to get close to the T. rex," you tell a zookeeper nearby. "We can activate its Sleep Collar!"

The zookeeper thinks for a moment before replying.

"I have two ideas," he says. "We could use the feeding crane to lift you up above the dino so you can slip a rope around it to tie it up. Or, we could put sleeping pills into some meat and hope the T. rex eats it and falls asleep. We use pills like this when we have to clean the tigers' teeth!"

"I don't want to be dangled above the dino," Maria says, clutching your hand. It does sound scary, but since the T. rex just ate the tigers' dinner, it probably isn't too hungry.

If you decide you want to lasso the T. rex from the food crane, turn to the next page.

If you think that putting sleeping pills in the food is a better idea, turn to page 34.

Just a few minutes later, you're in a safety harness dangling from a feeding crane so you can slip a rope around the neck of the escaped Tyrannosaurus rex. You aren't sure it was the best decision, but it's too late to change your mind.

Turn to page 20.

Maybe running straight at a maddened Tyrannosaurus rex is not the smartest thing you have ever done, even if it is a baby, but it is the bravest.

"Yahhhhh!!!!!" you yell, waving the Sleep Collar Activator and punching the SLEEP NOW button. Nothing happens.

You dodge a swipe from the T. rex's tiny arms, and then you turn and run the other way. The T. rex chases after you, so you keep punching SLEEP NOW.

Turn to page 30.

A Vid-Stream news crew arrives and asks you questions while filming everything.

"How does it feel to be dangling over the most fearsome of beasts?" a woman with a microphone asks you.

"Please, be quiet!" Maria tells everyone before you can answer. "It looks like it's falling asleep by itself!" she says, pointing at the T. rex.

"Easy now," the zookeeper says as he operates the crane, moving you closer to the T. rex.

Everyone holds their breath as the dino turns around three times and settles down on the tigers' sunning rock. You sway in the breeze above the moat.

The zookeeper moves you even closer. Now you are right above the dinosaur, and the rope lasso is dangling over its huge nose. You can smell and feel the breath of the baby Tyrant King of the Lizards.

A drop of sweat falls from your face.

Turn to the next page.

Before the drop lands, the T. rex is already up and leaping into the air at you! Its mouth is wide open.

Snap! You fall to the ground and look up.

The dinosaur is dangling by its teeth from the cable that was just holding you up!

Turn to page 25.

It grabs the unicorn's horn in its teeth and shakes its head like a dog with a bone. Then it tosses the unicorn into the air and gulps it down in one bite.

Turn to page 70.

"Run for the cave!" the zookeeper yells.

You glance over your shoulder. The cave is about thirty feet away. Can you make it? Is it deep enough to keep you safe?

The T. rex opens its jaws and falls to the ground. It then holds perfectly still. So do you.

"Use the Sleep Collar Activator!" Maria shouts.

You pull the activator from your pocket. The T. rex is watching you. To use the activator, you will have to get close to its sharp teeth and claws, but this may be your best chance.

If you decide to make a run for the cave, turn to the next page.

If you want to try to use the Sleep Collar Activator, turn to page 19.

You break for the cave, and the T. rex runs after you. Your heart is beating fast, and people are screaming. You have to make it to the cave before the dino does.

Roar!

The T. rex snaps at you as you dive under the thick rock ledge, and you drop the activator. You can smell the dino's bad breath on your face as you scoot back as far as you can into the cave.

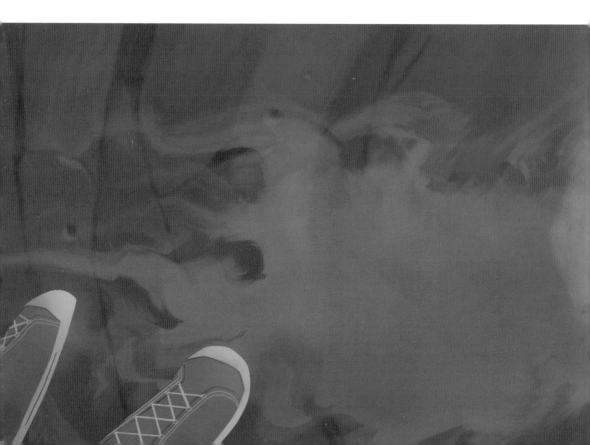

Its head is too big to get into the opening, and its little arms barely reach into the entrance. After a few minutes, it goes away. Then you hear a helicopter.

"Do not come out!" a voice from the chopper yells. "The T. rex is right outside the cave!"

Rocks poke your back, but you stay put. Why did you choose to be dangled over a dinosaur like a worm on a hook?

Turn to the next page.

The Sleep Collar Activator is still on the ground by the cave entrance. There is no way you could make it there in time to use it. Your leg cramps from being wedged into such a small spot.

Moving as slowly and quietly as possible, you stretch out your leg.

Suddenly the T. rex's tail swings into the cave beside you. The very tip of its tail hits you and sends you flying. You tumble out into the dirt and onto your belly. The activator is twenty feet away, and you speed-crawl toward it. The T. rex runs at you.

Crunch!

Go on to the next page.

The T. rex stomps on the activator and then gives you the scariest smile you have ever seen.

Boom!

Two rocket-powered nets from the helicopter hit the T. rex. Its arms and legs get tangled in the nets. After a minute it gives up and sits down. You close your eyes and sigh in relief. That was too close!

The End

Then you hear a bark—it's Homer! He's up in a tree only a few feet away. You scramble up the tree and hope the dino is a bad climber.

The T. rex runs straight at the tree, opens its mouth, and bites the tree trunk in half.

Crunch!

The tree falls, but luckily it falls onto a larger tree. You and Homer both leap into the bigger tree.

Turn to page 32.

What about the ring toss? No. Slide? No. Funhouse? Yes, but it's too far away. That leaves the squirt gun balloon-pop race, or the ice rink. Maybe you can scare it away with a squirt gun or hide in the giant stuffed animals at the balloon game. It's not a great plan, but the ice rink is farther away.

If you try to scare the T. rex using the balloon game, turn to page 42.

If you think the ice rink is the better bet, turn to page 68.

From high in the tree, you see a group of security people from the Dino Lab with stun guns crossing the moat.

"Help!" you yell, hoping that they reach you quickly. The T. rex opens its mouth wide to bite into your tree. Homer holds onto your shirt with his teeth while you reach down as close as you can and push the SLEEP NOW button frantically.

The baby T. rex's huge eyelids shut like double garage doors. It topples over head first, asleep.

You and Homer have saved the day!

The End

"Don't worry, this will work. I read about it in a book once," the zookeeper says, leading you to the zoo's veterinary hospital. He finds a bag full of blue capsules the size of hot dogs. Stuffing the capsules into a huge hunk of meat is kind of gross, but you help do it anyway.

Go on to the next page.

Then, using the food crane, the zookeeper swings the meat over the moat. The T. rex leaps into the air and gulps the chunk of meat down in one bite.

Turn to the next page.

"How long before it starts working?" you ask.

"Not long!" the zookeeper says.

But it does take a long time. The T. rex runs around the habitat. You think it looks mad, but it is not trying to escape. You wonder where the tigers are hiding. Finally, the dino settles down and curls up, sort of like a cat, with its giant head tucked under its tail. It looks like it's asleep.

Go on to the next page.

A bunch of security people from the Dino Lab arrive to help. They slowly cross the moat on ladders, but the T. rex keeps snoozing. You hold your breath as they get close enough to throw their thick nets over it.

Whip!
Spring!
Crash!

Turn to the next page.

"It was faking!" The zookeeper yells. "Watch out!" The T. rex whips its head in one direction and its thick tail in the other, knocking down all of the security people at once. Then in one smooth motion, it leaps straight toward you and lands on top of the ambulance.

Go on to the next page.

Everyone else is running away, and you think that is probably a good idea. You head toward the games and rides area of the park, thinking there might be a safe hiding spot. You hear the T. rex following you.

You look around frantically, but you don't see a good place to hide. The carousel might work to confuse the dino, but it isn't running right now. The bumper cars would slow it down, but only for a minute. The teacup ride would just make you into an easy meal!

Turn to page 31.

"Anything else you can tell us about Stegosauruses, Gerald?" Maria asks as you exit the automatic doors from the Dino Lab to the parking lot. Your aunt and Dr. Treeswinger are still helping Dr. Finjump. One of his flippers got cut on the broken glass from his tank.

"Well, basically, she just eats and sleeps," Gerald says. "And goes to the bathroom. A lot."

"Gross!" you say.

"Nana says that's not gross, it's just part of nature." Maria says.

"Look, there it is!" you yell. The baby Stegosaurus smashes through the parking lot gate and heads onto the main road leading downtown.

The parking lot attendant comes out of the booth, looks at the escaped dinosaur, and runs the other way. You feel like doing the same, but you grab Maria's hand and move forward.

"We have to get to it before something bad happens!"

Go on to the next page.

As you say that, you hear a loud crash.

"I think something bad just happened," Gerald says.

Turn to page 46.

You jump over the counter of the balloon game and grab one of the squirt guns. You point it at the T. rex and pull the squirt-trigger, but nothing happens.

The dino comes closer. Then you hear a bark–it's Homer! He found the "ON" switch under the counter. He bats it with his paw, and you try squirting again.

"Take that rot-breath!" you yell, as water shoots right up the dinner-plate-sized nostril of the baby T. rex. It gives an enormous sneeze and tries to scratch at its nose with its little arms. You scramble to the back of the game stall and burrow into a pile of stuffed animal prizes.

"Get away! Shoo! No one wants you here!" you hear someone shout.

Oh no! That's Maria yelling at the T. rex! You can't let her get hurt.

You start throwing stuffed animals at the T. rex's back to distract it from Maria. It doesn't notice the little ones, but it turns around when you hit it in the face with a purple unicorn.

Turn to page 24.

"Come on, Maria, let's go find the baby Stegosaurus!"

"It didn't look like a baby to me," Maria says. "Babies are cute little things that smell nice. This one has all sorts of sharp pointy-jabby things."

"The jabby things on its back are called 'scutes,'" you say, using your I-know-so-much voice. "Besides, I remember when you were a baby, and trust me, you smelled stinky way more than you smelled nice. But you and Gerald are right—those spikes could hurt someone."

"Besides," Gerald says, joining your conversation, "the Stegosaurus is known for not being the brightest sandwich in the lunchbox. Its brain is the size of a walnut!"

"I think you mean 'not the brightest light bulb in the box,'" you say. "And the Stegosaurus's brain is more the size and shape of a bent hot dog, but point taken."

Turn to page 40.

You follow claw marks on the pavement leading away from the parking lot.

"I bet it's headed to the Downtown Mega-Fun Completo-Mall!" says Maria. "That place is crazy enough without a dinosaur."

"I'm not allowed in there anymore," Gerald says. "Ever since the whole exploding rat incident in the movie theater. Speaking of the theater, Shelly might want to take a nap in there since it's so dark and cool."

"Wait, who's Shelly? We'll get to the exploding rat thing later," you say.

"Shelly is the Stegosaurus, of course!" Gerald says, making a crazy-swirl at his temple and grinning at Maria. "I guess she might go to the food court, but my bet is on the theater."

If you think the Stegosaurus is napping in the darkness of the movie theater, turn to page 48.

If you want to look for the baby Stegosaurus in the food court, turn to page 58.

"Gerald, you stay here with Shelly! Maria's plan is better than mine. We'll be back with pillows and cushions."

"If you go to Pillow World, can you pick up my special order Ninja Dog pillow?" Gerald asks. "I haven't been able to get it since the exploding rat incident."

"Okay," you sigh. "But where IS Pillow World?"

"It's right next door!" Maria says, grabbing your hand and pulling you along.

Turn to page 52.

People scream and run out of the theater as you are trying to enter.

Go on to the next page.

"I think we're going in the right direction," Gerald says. Someone grabs Gerald by his shoulders and screams in his face.

"Run! A dragon got loose from one of the movies! It's got huge fangs and it breathes fire and shoots lasers from it ears!"

"Settle down," Gerald says to the man. "It's just an escaped baby dinosaur, nothing to get upset about. Look! There's Shelly! Hi Shelly! Calm down! I'll get you a cycad leaf!"

From under his lab coat, Gerald pulls out a leafy branch that looks like it came from a palm tree. He waves it in the air and runs toward the Stegosaurus.

"Cycad?" Maria says.

"Cycads are plants that also lived millions of years ago—primo dino food," you say.

Turn to the next page.

Shelly has her front feet up on the counter of the concession stand. She is giving a low humming noise that you think sounds happy as she takes bites of popcorn straight out of the popcorn machine. The top of the machine is knocked off, and Shelly is munching away. She doesn't even look at Gerald and his cycad leaf.

"C'mon, Pumpkin," Gerald says in a baby voice. "Have a nice cycad leaf!"

"Watch out, Gerald!" Maria says as Shelly swings her tail absentmindedly. She has a chair cushion stuck to the spikes on her tail, and it knocks Gerald over.

"Lady Pompadour Reflection HardSHELL! You are very bad! Stop that at once!" Gerald says from the floor.

Shelly glances at Gerald for a microsecond and then goes back to her popcorn.

"I have an idea," you say. "We could lure Shelly into the Bungee Holo-Theater using candy. She's almost done with the popcorn."

"Let's throw more pillows and cushions on her so her spikes can't hurt anyone else. Besides, Gerald said she likes to sleep," Maria says.

If you like Maria's plan to use cushions and pillows to make Shelly less dangerous, turn to page 47.

If try to lure Shelly into the Bungee Holo-Theater, turn to page 54.

A few minutes later, you run back to the theater. You can't really see well because of the stack of pillows you are carrying.

You find Shelly at the other end of the theater lobby, with Gerald dancing around her trying to get her to fall asleep. You and Maria pile pillows on all of Shelly's sharp points, and by the time you are finished, Shelly has curled up and is snoozing.

"May as well join her," you say, lying down on the soft pillows next to Shelly. Maria jumps on you and hits you with one of the pillows.

"Hey, where's my Ninja Dog pillow?" Gerald says.

"Oops, we forgot it!" you say. "But why don't you tell us about that exploding rat incident?"

The End

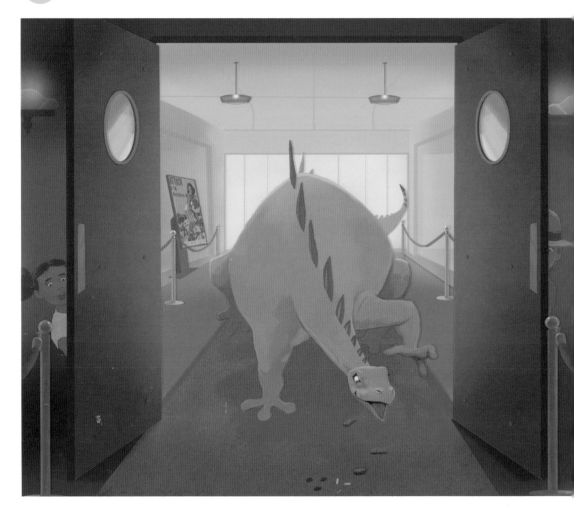

"My dad used this trick when I was a kid," Gerald says, as he lays down a trail of candy bars leading into the Bungee Holo-Theater.

Go on to the next page.

"But instead of candy, we used cat food. And instead of an escaped baby dinosaur in a mall movie theater, we had a skunk in our kitchen."

"Well I hope it works," you tell Gerald.

Shelly finishes the last of the popcorn and then moves on to the candy leading to the Bungee Holo-Theater. You've only been to a virtual reality movie in here once, but it was pretty amazing.

Shelly pauses by the door to the theater and looks around.

"Come on, Shelly, come on!" Maria whispers.

Then she eases through the door to get the next batch of candy. You shut the door behind her.

Turn to the next page.

It is dark in the Bungee Holo-Theater, and it smells like spilled soda and baby dinosaur. Suddenly Shelly makes a scared bellowing noise that sounds like a car alarm system being eaten.

"It's okay, Shelly! You're not going to get hurt!" Maria says, running toward a big dark shape bobbing in the air. When your eyes adjust to the darkness, you see why Shelly is so scared! She is completely tangled up in all of the bungee cables hanging from the ceiling. The more she tries to get free, the more she bounces and gets tangled up!

Maria runs up to Shelly and pets her face. Shelly stops bellowing and gives Maria a sloppy lick on her face with her big dino tongue.

"Yuck!" Maria says. "Now I smell like dino burps!"

"Well at least she'll stay put until the Dino Lab team gets here!" you say with relief.

The End

"I'm hungry anyway," you say. "Let's look for Shelly at the food court!"

"I looove smoothies," Gerald says to no one in particular.

When you get to the food court, you can tell that Shelly has been through here. The salad bar is tossed all over the floor, and pools of dressing make the floor slippery. The sushi station is a complete mess.

"The dinosaur ate a whole bucket of hot wasabi paste," a woman sitting at a nearby table tells you. "It started to sneeze, and sushi rolls went flying!"

"Thanks," you say. "Any idea where Shelly—I mean the dinosaur—went?

"Just follow the destruction!" she says, waving her hand. "It shouldn't be hard."

She's right. It is not hard to track Shelly down. But when you find her, you almost wish you hadn't. Shelly is napping in the middle of the grand showroom of The Elf Lord's Crystal Cave Emporium of Sacred Sculpture and Stemware!

Turn to the next page.

"Oh, I've always wanted to go here!" Gerald says loudly. "But it's supposed to be out-of-this-world expensive. More than an Assistant Lab Rat—I mean, Assistant Exploding Ratbatory—oh never mind! It's more than I can afford!"

Go on to the next page.

While you watch, Shelly jumps up from her sleep. She thrashes her tail around and knocks a life-size crystal statue of a wizard to the ground. The statue shatters into 789 pieces.

"I was a afraid of this," Gerald says. "I think Shell-Shell has a tummy ache. A widdle tummy-wummy upsy-setsy! It makes her grumpy."

"How do we get Shelly out of there without causing more damage?" you ask.

"I don't have any ideas," Gerald says. "Actually, I have two ideas. We could get some charcoal to soothe her tummy. Or maybe we could sing her one of her mama dino's lullabies. Other than that, not a single idea!"

If you want sing lullabies to Shelly to calm her down, turn to the next page.

If you decide you want to look for charcoal to soothe her stomach, turn to page 66.

"OK! From the top! And a one and a two and a three...PUUUUM-oohhh-PLOOOOMP," Gerald sings while waving his arms around as though he is conducting a symphony orchestra.

"This time with FEELING!" Gerald says. "PLOOOOP-PLOOOP! Plop-PLOOP!"

You and Maria both start to laugh.

Shelly turns to look at the two of you laughing. She smashes her tail into more valuable works of crystal art. A snowy owl in flight and a rearing horse now lay shattered on the floor next to the wizard.

"Come on, Shell-Shell," Maria says softly. "No more smashing."

Shelly starts to walk toward you but then stops and looks up.

You look up too. Then you hear it.

Turn to page 64.

"Thank you for taking care of the Stegosaurus situation," the team leader tells you as they are leaving with Shelly. "You're a real hero!"

You are beaming with pride when someone tugs your arm.

"Who's going to pay for my crystal statues!?" says a small man who looks like an elf. "It took two years to carve that owl. Two years!!!"

"I don't know," you say. "I'm sorry about your owl, but I was just trying to help. It's not my Stegosaurus!"

"That may be," the elf-man replies, "but you look like just the right person to deal with the little *present* your dinosaur friend left behind." He points to a big pile of dino poo.

Oh no! you think. This is worse than cleaning up the broken glass.

"I told you she goes to the bathroom a lot!" Gerald says.

"Come on Gerald," you say. "Help me clean this up. Or I'm going to tell Aunt Sarah about the exploding rat incident!"

The End

CREEE-AWKKKKKKK!

"That's the cry of the Pteranodon!" you tell Maria.

A black shadow blots out the sun from the skylights.

Crash!

The Pteranodon crashes down through the skylight.

Whummph! It lands right between you, Maria, and Gerald.

"Oh, right, silly me!" Gerald says. "That wasn't the Stegosaurus lullaby, it was the Pteranodon dinner call!"

"Thanks Gerald," you say. "Now we have to get TWO dinos back to the lab!"

The End

Since it is summer, finding a bag of charcoal should be easy. You head toward the mall hardware store, but before you get very far, you are surprised to see your dog Homer running right at you! And he is holding a bag of charcoal in his teeth.

"Homer! Did you follow us all the way from home?" you say. He barks and gives you a satisfying lick.

"I guess he really wanted to see the dinos!" Maria says.

Shelly still seems a bit agitated. You give the charcoal to Gerald, and he pushes the open bag through the doorway of the Crystal Cave Emporium. Shelly immediately gobbles down the briquettes, then she burps and settles down looking happy. Within a few minutes, the team from the Dino Lab arrives to bring her back home.

Turn to page 63.

You break for the ice rink. The T. rex is running straight at you with its head down like a battering ram.

You rush through the doors to the ice rink and slam them shut behind you. You look around frantically for something to bar the door. *Crash!* The T. rex smashes in and wiggles its body through the doorway.

You scramble out onto the ice and slide away from the T. rex as fast as you can without falling.

You look back and see the T. rex come toward you on the ice. It wobbles and almost falls, but then an amazing thing happens. The T. rex stops chasing you and starts sliding around the ice like a professional figure skater! It looks like it's having a lot of fun.

When the Dino Lab security crew arrives to take it back home, you feel a little sad. You decide you will ask Aunt Sarah about adding an ice rink to the habitat back at the lab.

The End

"Give it another toy!" Maria says.

You throw a pink gorilla at it next. The T. rex starts making happy hooting noises as it chomps on the gorilla.

By the time the Dino Lab security crew arrives, the T. rex has actually settled down and fallen asleep with the stuffed gorilla still in its mouth.

"I think it just wanted a chew toy," Maria says. You and Homer have to agree.

The End

ABOUT THE AUTHOR

After graduating from Williams College with a degree specializing in Ancient History, **Anson Montgomery** spent ten years founding and working in technology-related companies, as well as working as a freelance journalist for financial and local publications. He is the author of a number of books in the original *Choose Your Own Adventure* series, including *Everest Adventure, Snowboard Racer, Moon Quest* (reissued in 2008 by Chooseco), and *CyberHacker,* as well as two volumes of *Choose Your Own Adventure — The Golden Path*, part of a three volume series. Anson lives in Warren, Vermont with his wife, Rebecca, and his two daughters, Avery and Lila.

ABOUT THE ILLUSTRATOR

Keith Newton began his art career in the theater as a set painter. Having talent and a strong desire to paint portraits, he moved to New York and studied fine art at the Art Students League. Keith has won numerous awards in art such as The Grumbacher Gold Medallion and Salmagundi Award for Pastel. He soon began illustrating and was hired by Disney Feature Animation where he worked on such films as *Pocahontas* and *Mulan* as a background artist. Keith also designed color models for sculptures at Disney Animal Kingdom and has animated commercials for Euro Disney. Today, Keith Newton freelances from his home and teaches entertainment illustration at The College for Creative Studies in Detroit. He is married and has two daughters.

For games, activities and other fun stuff, or to write to Anson Montgomery, visit us online at www.cyoa.com